To Steven, Brian
and Megan—M.M.

For Kristi—D.C.

Text copyright © 1983 by Michaela Muntean.
Illustrations copyright © 1983 by Doug Cushman.
All rights reserved.
Printed in the United States of America.
10 9 8 7 6 5 4 3 2

Library of Congress Cataloging in Publication Data
Muntean, Michaela.
   Bicycle Bear.
   Summary: Items are never too big or too small—
Bicycle Bear delivers them all.
   [1. Delivery of goods—Fiction.   2. Bears—Fiction.
3. Stories in rhyme]   I. Cushman, Doug, ill.
II. Title.
PZ8.3.M89Bi   1983   [E]   83-3980
ISBN 0-8193-1103-0

A Parents Magazine
READ ALOUD Original.

Bicycle Bear

by Michaela Muntean
pictures by Doug Cushman

Parents Magazine Press • New York

When you want to send a package,
when you want to send a hug,
when you want to send some flowers,
or an Oriental rug...

When it won't fit in the mailbox,
when the postman says *no way,*
when it absolutely has to be there
on that very day...

Call Bicycle Bear!
Oh, Bicycle Bear!
Just give him a ring
and he'll be there.

He'll deliver green pickles,
deliver sweet jams,
deliver your kisses,
and sing telegrams.

But the most surprising thing,
you will hear him say,
came upon a Tuesday,
the twenty-first of May.

The day began quite normally
when he woke up at dawn.
He stretched a bear-size stretch.
He yawned a bear-size yawn.

He hopped onto his bicycle
and off to work he went.
He had a long, long list of things
that needed to be sent.

The first two things were pizzas.
He picked them up with ease.
One was topped with sausage,
and one had extra cheese.

A bunch of roses followed,
then a kitten in a box,
two bowls of shiny goldfish,
a pair of purple socks...

two hats with fuzzy pompons,
a suitcase filled with shoes,
a postcard with a picture
of New York City views.

The list went on and on
and so did Bicycle Bear,
collecting plants and packages
and a great big rocking chair.

"One more stop," said Bicycle Bear.
"I hope it's something small.
A feather would be very nice,
or a little Ping Pong ball."

But at the home of Ima Goose
he got a big surprise.
It was so big that Bicycle Bear
could not believe his eyes!

"Oh, yes, indeed," said Ima.
"I always try to send
something big and different
to Eleanor, my friend."

"That is fine," said Bicycle Bear,
who hemmed and hawed a bit.
"The only problem is," he said,
"I don't know where he'll fit."

He thought a while, then set to work.
He tried a lot of things.
He wrapped up that big Birthday Moose
with ribbons, bows and strings.

He put him in a bag.
He put him in a box.

He put him in
a big wood crate
and locked it
with two locks.

But no matter what he tried
it kept on coming loose.
"There's got to be a way," he said,
"to take a Birthday Moose."

He wondered how to move him
without boxes, bags or crates.
Then all at once he shouted out...

"Not only will you get there,
but you'll be helping me.
It won't be hard for you to hold
a thing, or two, or three."

And so from town to town they went.
They traveled here and there
delivering the goldfish,
delivering the chair,

delivering the roses,
the hats and pizzas, too.
"When we're done," said Bicycle Bear,
"I must deliver *you!*"

He found the house of Eleanor
and called, "Delivery!"
But there was no one home.
Oh, where could Eleanor be?

"Now what," he mumbled to himself
and scratched his furry head.
Then he saw the posted note
and this is what it said:

He followed the directions.
He found the yellow door.
Behind it was a party
and there was Eleanor.

It was her birthday party!
The guests were celebrating.
Some of them were eating cake...

"Oh, my stars!" cried Eleanor.
"Is it true? Oh, can it be?
Is this moose on rollerskates
a birthday gift for me?"

"Why, yes," said Bicycle Bear,
"from your good friend, Ima Goose.
She sends her warmest wishes
with this handsome Birthday Moose."

"Oh what a thoughtful gift!
Now I'd like it if you'd take
a thank you note to Ima.
But first, please have some cake."

"I'm happy to do both,"
said Bicycle Bear with a smile.
And so he had some birthday cake
and skated for a while.

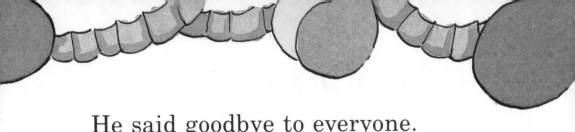

He said goodbye to everyone.
He thanked the Birthday Moose.
"And now I'll be returning
to the home of Ima Goose."

He hopped onto his bicycle
and back to work he went.
There was a special thank you note
that needed to be sent!

So, when you want to send a package
or a turtle or a fish.
When you want to send a tuba,
or anything you wish...

Call Bicycle Bear!
Oh, Bicycle Bear!
Just give him a ring
and he'll be there.

No job is too big.
No job is too small.
Bicycle Bear will
deliver it all!

About the author

MICHAELA MUNTEAN is the eldest of seven children who like to give each other unusual birthday gifts. "But my brothers and sisters live all over the country and sending the gifts isn't easy." So Ms. Muntean started thinking of funny ways to send her gifts and BICYCLE BEAR was born.

Michaela Muntean has written three other books for Parents Magazine Press, including THE VERY BUMPY BUS RIDE. She lives in New York City.

About the Artist

DOUG CUSHMAN is the illustrator of many children's books. He says he especially enjoyed working on BICYCLE BEAR because it's so silly. "Also, Birthday Moose reminds me of a dog I know."

Mr. Cushman lives in New Haven, Connecticut. In addition to illustrating, he enjoys writing, cooking, and playing tennis. This is his first book for Parents Magazine Press.